The Adventures of
CAP'N O.G. READMORE

to the tune of "The Cat Came Back"

adapted by
FRAN MANUSHKIN

illustrated by
MANNY CAMPANA

SCHOLASTIC INC.
New York Toronto London Auckland Sydney Tokyo

**Based on the character developed by ABC Entertainment
in cooperation with the Library of Congress**

ISBN 0-590-33246-5

12 11 10 9 8 7 6 5 4 3 2 1   4   4 5 6 7 8 / 8
Printed in the U.S.A.   24

A cat lived in an alley.
O.G. Readmore was his name.
Listen to the story
of how he rose to fame.

He taught himself the alphabet
from A to X Y Z.
"Now that I can read," he said,
"I'll join the library!"

"No card for you," the lady said.
"For all I know, you'll eat it."
But O.G. begged her for a book.
He said, "I won't mistreat it."

"Let me introduce myself:
I am the reading cat.
And I'll be back tomorrow
and the next day after that."

　　　And...

The cat came back
to take another book out.
The cat came back
the very next day.
The cat came back.
The cat was on the lookout
for a book to read.
He just couldn't stay away.

One day O.G. was hungry.
He had nothing left to eat.
The temperature was soaring.
He was gasping from the heat.

Now he could read the sign that said:
ALL CATS CAN EAT HERE—**FREE!**
He lapped up 18 ice-cream cones
and purred, "How cool of me!"

And...

The cat came back
to take another book out.
The cat came back
the very next day.
The cat came back.
The cat was on the lookout
for a book to read.
He just couldn't stay away.

One night there were some fireworks
for all the town to see.
A rocket went astray and landed
near some TNT.

The cap'n knew from what he'd read
that TNT meant trouble.
He grabbed the box and leaped
into the water on the double.

And...

The cat came back
to take another book out.
The cat came back
the very next day.
The cat came back.
The cat was on the lookout
for a book to read.
He just couldn't stay away.

feline feasts
Your cat can swim
GREAT FISH DISHES
See The World by Boat
MOBY CAT
WHALES, SHARKS AND ANIMALS OF THE SEA
SAILING

O.G. was sailing on a ship
and thought he'd take a swim.
Ooooops! Suddenly a sneaky shark
came racing after him.

Quick! O.G. found his trusty book.
It told him, "Without fail,
whenever sharks swim after you,
just whistle for a whale."

And...

The cat came back
to take another book out.
The cat came back
the very next day.
The cat came back.
The cat was on the lookout
for a book to read.
He just couldn't stay away.

The cap'n took a camping trip
and climbed a mountain high.
He stopped to rest and read and lunch
on trout and apple pie.

When—*CRASH!*—There was an avalanche!
The boulders were no joke.
He turned to page one hundred three,
then wrote, "PLEASE HELP!" in smoke.

And...

The cat came back
to take another book out.
The cat came back
the very next day.
The cat came back.
The cat was on the lookout
for a book to read.
He just couldn't stay away.

The cap'n thought he'd take a trip
to outer space and back.
The rocket got in trouble.
The computers all went black!

But O.G. knew just what to do—
he read the fix-it guide.
He brought the rocket back on course
and then had quite a ride.

   And...

The cat came back
to take another book out.
The cat came back
the very next day.
The cat came back.
The cat was on the lookout
for a book to read.
He just couldn't stay away.

O.G. went skating in the woods
as fast as he could spin,
when he saw something in a tree
that made him stop and grin:

Three kittens holding up a sign,
PLEASE SAVE US IF YOU CAN.
Right then and there that trusty cat
became a family man!

And...

The cat came back
to take another book out.
The cat came back
the very next day.
The cat came back.
The cat was on the lookout
for a book to read.
He just couldn't stay away.

The Cat Came Back

One day O. G. was hun-gry. He had noth-ing left to eat.__ The

tem-per-a-ture was soar-ing. He was gasp-ing from the heat. Now

he could read the sign that said: ALL CATS CAN EAT HERE—FREE! He

lapped up eigh-teen ice cream cones and purred. "How cool of me!"

Chorus

And the cat came back to take an-oth-er book out. Oh, the

cat came back the ver-y next day. The cat came back. The

cat was on the look-out for a book to read. He just could-n't stay a-way.